Your Auntie Loves You!

by Sally Helmick North

This book is a special reminder...

your auntie loves you!

Your auntie loves you,
that's so true...

more than a fishie,
pink and blue.

More than a zebra,
with a polka-dot coat...

or a little pirate ducky,
on a teeny, tiny boat!

More than a penguin, singing a song...

or a cute little fly,
who is buzzing right along!

More than a king crab,
laying in the sun...

or a bullfrog waiter,

serving everyone!

Your auntie loves you,
that you'll see...

more than a doggie,

happy as can be!

More than a hippo,
wearing a hat...

or a red and black tie

on a big, fat cat!

More than a starfish, jumping in the sand...

or a crazy alligator, in a rock and roll band!

More than a bunny,
with a Superman suit...

or a really tall giraffe!

That would surely be a hoot!

When the stars shine bright...

or the sky is blue...

Your auntie really loves you...

That is TRUE! TRUE! TRUE!

Your Auntie Loves You!
Copyright ©2016 by Sally Helmick North

Sally was born in Jackson, Michigan. She has lived all over the country with her husband, Fred. They have 3 grown children, and they all live in Louisville, KY. She has written over 30 children's books and had her first book published in 2000. Sneaky Snail Stories are all sweet and simple rhyming books with really cute illustrations. You can see all the Sneaky Snail Stories at: www. sneakysnailstories.com

Other books by Sally:

No Pancakes for Puppy
Grandma and Grandpa Love You
Your Aunt Loves You
The Best Day

Emma's Hilarious Horse Book (personalized for boys or girls with cats, dogs, penguins or frogs)
Emma, the Super, Amazing, Awesome, Intelligent, Girly-Girl (personalized)
Noah the Basketball Star (personalized for several sports for boys or girls)
Noah's Very Own Cook Book (personalized for boys or girls)
Grandma and Grandpa Love Emma (personalized from any relative for boys or girls)
Emma Turns One! (personalized for boys or girls ages 1-6)   and many more....

website: www.sneakysnailstories.com   facebook: Sneaky Snail Stories
Etsy: (search for) thesneakysnailstore   Amazon: (search for) Sally Helmick North

See all the Sneaky Snail Stories at: www.sneakysnailstories.com

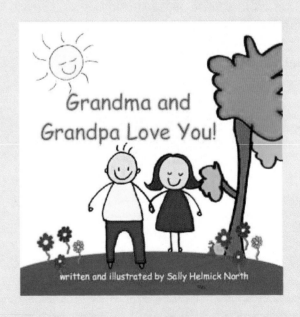

Merry Christmas Lennox!
Your Auntie Loves you so much!

Love,
Aunt Jess
XOXOXO

12-2016

Made in the USA
Lexington, KY
17 December 2016